For Jo, with all my love.
T. B.

To Sam.
R. B.

First edition for the United States, its territories and dependencies and Canada
published in 2005 by Barron's Educational Series, Inc.

First published in Great Britain in 2004 by Gullane Children's Books, an imprint of Pinwheel Limited,
259-269 Old Marylebone Road, London, NW1 5XJ

Text © Tony Bonning 2004
Illustrations © Rosalind Beardshaw 2004

All inquiries should be addressed to:
Barron's Educational Series, Inc.
250 Wireless Blvd.
Hauppauge, NY 11788
**www.barronseduc.com**

International Standard Book No.: 0-7641-5824-4

Library of Congress Catalog No.: 2004107926

Printed and bound in China
9 8 7 6 5 4 3 2 1

# Snog the Frog

Tony Bonning • Rosalind Beardshaw

**BARRON'S**

Beside a grand and
majestic castle was a pond,

and at the bottom
of this cool, clear pond
lived Snog the Frog.

Snog the Frog climbed on his log and said, "Today is my birthday, and today I wish to feel like a prince. And to be a prince I need a kiss!"

With that in mind, he leapt onto the
land and went

HOPPITY HOPPITY HOPPITY HOP,

until who should he meet, but Cow.

"Oh, Cowy Cow Cow! I wish to feel like a prince.
Pucker up your lovely lips and give me a kiss!"

"Who? You? Moo! No! Now go!"
"Oh! Just one?"
"No, go!"
And with that he went . . .

HOPPITY HOPPITY HOPPITY HOP,
until who should he meet, but Sheep.

"Oh, Sheepy Sheep Sheep! I wish to feel like a
prince. Send those sheepish lips my way and give me a kiss."
"Me? Baa! Nah! No!"
"Oh! Perhaps a peck?"
"Nooo, go!"

So with that, Snog the Frog went

HOPPITY

HOPPITY

HOPPITY HOP,

until who should he meet,
but Snake.

"Oh, Snakey Snake Snake! I wish to feel like a prince.
Press those lean lips on mine and give me a kiss."
"A kiss, hissss, take this!"
"Oh no! I'll give that a miss."

And with this, he went HOPPITY HOPPITY HOPPITY HOP, until who should he meet, but Pig.

"Oh, Hoggy Hog Hog, give this Froggy Frog Frog a snoggy snog snog."
"What! Snort! I'd never kiss your sort."
"Spoilsport."

And with that, Snog the Frog went
HOPPITY
HOPPITY
HOPPITY HOP,

until who should he meet, but . . .

# ...Princess!

"Oh, Princess, Your Highness, such happiness would I possess were you to kiss me but once. Make me feel like a prince."

"Oh!" said the Princess, "I've read about this in fairy tales. One kiss and you turn into a prince."

And with that, she lifted Snog the Frog
and gave him a kiss.

"Alas, something is amiss.
The kiss has not turned you into a prince."
"Again, again, just one." The deed was done but . . .

**nothing!**

"Oh my!
Have one last try."
She did.

"I have tried once
and twice more since,
but you have not
become a prince."

**"No!"**
said Snog the Frog . . .